WHERE DO MY BROTHER AND SISTER GO?

MARIAN LOUISE CAMDEN, PSY. D.

Illustrated by JULIETH ECKERT

A story for blended family children whose siblings
have shared custody

Published by
Dawn & Dusk Publications, LLC

See Dr. Camden's other books for children at earthchildbooks.com:

An Earth Child's Book of the Year

An Earth Child's Book of Verse

If you find this book valuable, please consider spreading the word by writing a brief review on *amazon.com*. Thank you for supporting our passion for helping children and families.

--MLC and JE

For Sophie--and her big brother and sister.
with love from Dr. C.

I am Sophie and this is my house.

Here is my mommy.
She is cuddling our cat.

This is my daddy.
He is feeding our dog.

3

And here are my
brother and sister.
They are getting ready
to go away from our house
4 to have parenting time.

"What is parenting time?"
I wonder.

Sometimes
they call it
other things,
like "visitation,"
"spending the
weekend," or even
just "going to see
their dad."

I don't understand what this means. We have my daddy right here.

He plays with us a lot and he always says, "I love all my kids!"

6

My big brother and sister sometimes call him "Jim" or "Jim-Dad" and Mommy says he is really their stepdad.

Stepdad, I wonder? What is that? He just seems like a regular dad to me.

Yet, my big brother and sister
do have another daddy, one
they call their "real dad."
He is not my daddy.

I don't get into the car with him when he comes to pick them up. Mommy and I wave as they all drive away.

Now we are alone.

Where do my
brother and sister go?

Some things are fun
when they go away.

Mommy has more time
to play with me in the mornings.

11

She lets me take all the time I want to decide what clothes to wear.

After dinner, Daddy says,
"Your turn to choose what kind of ice cream
we have tonight, Soph." I always pick
the green kind with chocolate chips in it.

No waiting my turn when I play Dangerous Donkeys on the computer. I get all the turns myself, and nobody says, "Hurry up!"

Still, I miss my brother and sister. What do they eat for dinner? What games do they play over there?

At bedtime, Mommy reads me extra stories.

Daddy always sings my favorite song, the really long one with lots of verses about the green frog who marries a mouse.

Still, I miss my big brother and sister.

Where do they sleep?
What songs does that
other daddy sing to them?
18   Do they miss me, too?

After dinner on Sunday night, my brother and sister always come home.

"You're back!" I shout.
"Sophie!" they scream.
We hug until we fall on the floor
in a big, giggling kid-pile.

Mommy asks them,
"Did you have fun?"

Sometimes they had lots of fun,
watching a movie or going
swimming with their dad.
Just regular days are nice, too.

But the one thing they say every time is, "We missed you, Sophie!"

Then we eat their favorite kind of ice cream.
I wait my turn on the video game. And we all
run around making noise until Mommy
and Daddy tell us, "Quiet down!"
But they smile when they say it.
They know we love to have fun together.

In our family, whether we are together or apart, we all love each other, very, very much.

For Parents

by Marian Camden, Psy.D.
Licensed Psychologist

Blended or stepfamilies are on the rise, and increasing numbers of young children are being born into them. "Yours, mine, and ours" families are quickly becoming common. While many children's books have been written about divorce and about children of divorce adjusting to new blended or stepfamilies, few, if any, are available for the younger half-siblings born into these families. Both for better and worse, these "ours" children are in a unique position. As they mature, "ours" children become increasingly aware that their family is different from others.

On the one hand, young "ours" children enjoy the consistency and security of living in one home, with two parents in an intact relationship. Their parents are not new to caring for children and are often older, wiser, and better parents because of all they have gone through and learned themselves. As younger children, often significantly younger than their half-siblings, they often enjoy special attention and love from their older sisters and brothers — although jealousy from these older children is also not uncommon.

Yet, blended families are more complicated than simple nuclear families. Older siblings come and go, seemingly inexplicably. There is talk of, and often the limited presence of, their siblings' other parent. Terms like "parenting time," "ex," "divorce," "joint custody," and "half-sibling" confuse these young children. The young "ours" child often has the nagging sense that a lot has gone on in their family before he or she arrived on the scene. Some worry that their own intact family may split apart, and many feel unnecessary pressure and responsibility to please everyone, all the time.

Yet, young children do not easily express their feelings or ask their most heartfelt questions readily. Children three to eight think in concrete terms, and they often do not have the language skills to say or ask clearly about what is on their mind.

Many also have the feeling that they "shouldn't" ask questions about their parents' and siblings' pasts, especially if they sense their parents or sibs continue to feel tense, sad, or angry about all that has happened.

Parents can do a lot to help their young children understand and handle the complexities of their family life. Simply teaching children the words for various feelings and making it a practice to talk about them in everyday life can be a big help. Flashcards, picture books, even feelings words written on a beach ball and tossed back and forth can all be used to increase the young child's emotional literacy. As adults, expressing our own feelings simply and clearly provides good role modeling and reinforcement for children as well. Of course, this means having healthy ways ourselves to talk about and otherwise express emotions; and the focus should remain on meeting the children's needs above our own when they are around. When questions or feelings arise in your young child specific to the blended family, try to respond simply and directly. It is best to answer the actual question asked without going on into explanations beyond your child's understanding or interest. The classic funny story about this tendency we well-meaning adults have is little Billy asking his mother where he came from. After a long, awkward explanation of the facts of life, little Billy replies, "That's funny, Joey says he came from Boston." Simple is usually better. That said, do reassure your child that it is always okay to ask questions about anything he or she wonders about, and don't hesitate to answer at a level you think he or she will understand. There is nothing to keep secret, nothing to be ashamed of, and all of your child's questions deserve your attention.

Research tells us clearly that avoiding open conflict between divorced parents is vital to the psychological health and development of children of divorce. The same principle is true for "ours" children. Try to be matter of fact, even positive, about the reality that the older children have another parent and spend time with him or her regularly. Badmouthing your ex in front of the children never helps them and usually doesn't do you much good either. When you have worries or upset feelings to discuss about your ex, do it privately with your new partner, a trusted friend, or a psychologist, always out of earshot of the children. And don't think they can't hear or understand you in another room or if you are talking carefully on the telephone. Children hear and feel it all, like the proverbial little "sponges" they are.

Maintaining a good routine at home while the older children are gone is also helpful. Meal times, bath times, bedtime routines, and so on should remain essentially the same. Having the same expectations about rules and behavior is also wise. You can be sympathetic and understanding about your child's more sensitive feelings while the siblings are gone yet maintain reasonable order and behavior.

You may also want to build in something special for your child to anticipate that happens only when he or she is without the siblings. Children are often lonely when their siblings go away and they miss the fun and activity that goes on when they are all together. In this story, little Sophie gets more time with her parents, makes more choices, and enjoys more of her "turn" on the electronic games while her siblings are away. Increasing one-on-one time with parents helps with emotional security. Having more choices instills self-confidence and independence. And having more fun is, well, fun!

Parents in blended families need to take good care of themselves, as well. The children depend on you for everything, and that means you need to be in good shape, too. Take time to nurture your current relationship. Find ways both to grow and relax and have fun on your own and with friends. Being healthy, happy, and well-rounded is important for you as a person and a parent and is excellent role modeling for your children as well. As much as possible, live the life you hope they will live when they are adults. Finally, enjoy whatever is, whenever it is. When all your children are home and it's crazy and chaotic, take a deep breath and jump right in. When the older children are off with the other parent, relax a little, be grateful for the time off, and focus on loving up your young child, your partner, and yourself in special ways. Flexibility, acceptance, and a good sense of humor are keys to success in the special family you have created. A blended family is complicated and can be a lot of physical work and emotional effort, but, as you probably know already, the love and joy you experience together is just about the best thing ever. Enjoy!

Froggy Went A-Courtin'
(Ding Dang Dong Go the Wedding Bells)

Cheshire the cat lived over the hill.
Ding dang dong go the wedding bells.
The pretty little mouse lived under the mill.
Ding dang dong go the wedding bells.

Froggy went a courtin' and he did ride
Ding dang dong go the wedding bells,
He said Miss Mouse won't you be my bride?
Ding dang dong go the wedding bells.

Chorus: Here's to Cheshire, here's to cheese,
Here's to the pears and the apple trees,
And here's to the lovely strawberries.
Ding dang dong go the wedding bells.

I'll have to ask my old Aunt Rat,
Ding dang dong go the wedding bells,
Just what she does think of that.
Ding dang dong go the wedding bells.

Now Aunt Rat laughed till her face got red,
Ding dang dong go the wedding bells,
Just to think that a frog and a mouse should wed.
Ding dang dong go the wedding bells.
Chorus

Who's gonna weave that wedding gown?
Ding dang dong go the wedding bells,
Old Miss Spider from Pumpkin Town.
Ding dang dong go the wedding bells.

So break open the oysters and spill the champagne,
Ding dang dong go the wedding bells,
We're never gonna see such a party again.
Ding dang dong go the wedding bells.
Chorus
Oh, while they were going it hot and strong,
Ding dang dong go the wedding bells,
Chesire the cat came prowling along.
Ding dang dong go the wedding bells.

She sprang to the kitchen right out of the yard,
Ding dang dong go the wedding bells,
She didn't even have no invitation card.
Ding dang dong go the wedding bells.

Now this is the end of him and her.
Ding dang dong go the wedding bells.
Guess there won't be no tadpoles covered with fur.
Ding dang dong go the wedding bells.
Chorus

31

Dr. Marian Camden is a child and family psychologist specializing in divorce, stepfamily, and blended family matters. See camdencounseling.com. *Where Do My Brother and Sister Go?* is her third book for children. Dr. Camden lives and works in Colorado and loves to garden and to celebrate the earth. Her previous titles include *An Earth Child's Book of the Year* and *An Earth Child's Book of Verse*. See earthchildbooks.com.

Julieth Eckert is an accomplished Brazilian artist and illustrator. She has illustrated *Flying Beyond Our Wishes*, by Rayvhin Alejandra, and *Contos do Vovô*, by Ivoni Tacques, as well as covers for several Brazilian titles. In addition to her artistic work, Julieth is studying psychology. With a little half-brother of her own, Julieth has a special interest in blended and stepfamilies. She can be reached at julieth.be@gmail.com or at http://juliethbe.wix.com/julieth.

29291375R00023

Made in the USA
San Bernardino, CA
19 January 2016